MUSICAL ST

SONGS AND ACTIV

Ourselves

Cathy McCallum

A & C BLACK · LONDON

First published 2012 by A&C Black Publishers Ltd, an imprint of Bloomsbury
Publishing Plc.
50 Bedford Square, London, WC1B 3DP
© 2012

ISBN 978 1 4081 6561 4

Printed in China by South China Printing Company, Dongguan City, Guangdong
Teaching text © Cathy McCallum
Lyrics and melody for Stretch and wiggle, What shall we do with our friends today?,
Family song, Jump out of bed and Tick-tock © Cathy McCallum
Lyrics for Senses song and Can you play? © Cathy McCallum
Arrangements and sound engineering by Stephen Chadwick
Sound recording © 2012 A&C Black
March from *The Nutcracker* by Pyotr Ilyich Tchaikovsky, licensed courtesy of Naxos
Rights International

Cover design by Saffron Stocker
Cover and inside images © Shutterstock 2012
Series edited and developed by Stephanie Matthews
Designed by Saffron Stocker and Cathy Tincknell

Contents

Introduction

Musical Steps

Musical Steps began life in 2002 as parent and child music classes. The concept grew and, as we moved into nurseries, playgroups and children's centres, a very effective teaching method was developed. Experience showed that the simpler the songs and activities were, the better the children responded. Many of our most popular songs use only two or three different notes, and we concentrate on the basic 'building blocks' of music (just like learning letter sounds or counting from 1 to 10).

Who this book is for

Every child deserves to be introduced to music in a fun and accessible way, so if you work with young children this book is for you. If you already enjoy teaching music, this book will give you more ideas and help you to teach more effectively, and if you find teaching music a challenge, then you'll discover that it's not so difficult after all.

In many parts of the world, music-making is as natural and fundamental to daily life as talking, eating and sleeping. No one is labelled 'musical' or 'unmusical' and it's not left to specialists. If you can tell the difference between a high sound (like birdsong) and a low sound (like a bus engine) then you can teach the musical concept of 'high and low'. If you can tell when music is fast or slow or loud and quiet, then you can use the activities in this book.

How Musical Steps activities work

• Everything is very, very **simple** and at the correct musical level for young children.

• We use **fun** and games to teach important concepts.

• A large amount of **repetition** is built in.

• We **focus** on a small number of important musical concepts.

How to use this book

Use the CD to learn the songs yourself before introducing them to the children. There are three recordings of each song: the voice with backing track (VB), the backing track (B) and the voice-only track (V). Ideally you should sing without a backing track, as this will help the children to focus on the melody, and you will be able to adapt the songs more easily for teaching purposes (e.g. singing more slowly, adding more verses, or singing in different styles as described in the activities). Props and resources have been kept to a minimum, and consist of things you probably already have, or can easily make with the children. See p48 for books, music and websites to help you.

Tips on teaching the songs

Everything in this book is at the right musical level for the age group, so you can simply sing the songs and the children will be able to join in. There is no need to learn the words first, or tackle songs line by line. The children's confidence and competence will grow with familiarity, so a large amount of repetition is built into the activities, and the children will naturally pick up the songs and actions in their own time.

How does music help children develop?

It is well established that music plays a vital role in children's social, emotional and neurological development, but what will the children actually learn about music through this book? Here are the main musical skills and concepts that we focus on:

• keeping the beat (just as you do when you tap your foot along to music)

• fast and slow (tempo)

• loud and quiet (dynamics)

• high and low (pitch)

• structure (the shape of the music, e.g. verse and chorus, question and answer)

• timbre (the type of sound a voice or instrument produces)

Music is also a fun and accessible way to cover many other areas of learning, whichever curriculum or framework you are working with. Throughout this book you'll see abbreviations in the 'Focus' sections. For simplicity, these broadly refer to the three **prime** areas and the four **specific** areas of the English Early Years Foundation Stage framework:

Communication and language (CL)

The activities in this book help the children to develop their speaking and listening skills, and to practise following instructions.

Physical development (PD)

The children develop their fine motor and gross motor skills by playing percussion instruments in a controlled way and moving their bodies to the music.

Personal, social and emotional development (PSED)

The children learn to listen to one another, work together and take turns. They explore emotions by singing songs in different moods.

Literacy (L)

The constant use of rhyme in the activites prepares the children for reading and writing, and the children expand their vocabulary through song.

Mathematics (M)

Music teaches children about pattern, and there are many counting songs and activities throughout this book.

Understanding the world (UW)

The children learn about materials through making and playing instruments and listening to the sounds that different materials make.

Expressive arts and design (EAD)

Music-making encourages children to be imaginative and express themselves.

Music in the early years setting

This book is a starting point. Music should, and can easily be at the heart of teaching and learning. Here are some ways you can make music an integral part of your daily routine:

• Create a permanent music area where children can experiment, explore and listen to music. Include a selection of percussion instruments such as maracas, claves, finger cymbals and jingle bells. Making instruments is a great way to help children learn about materials and the sounds they make.

• Sing as much as you can throughout the day. For example, adapt 'What shall we do with our friends today?' (p18) for everyday questions: 'Archie, Archie, please say, what would you like for your snack today?'.

• Introduce 'tidy away' music. The children will soon get into the habit of tidying away when the music starts, without you having to use other methods to get their attention.

Safety tips

• watch noise levels – for enjoyment and for hearing safety

• whenever background music is suggested for painting or water activities, ensure that electrical equipment is kept safely away from water and wet hands

• play the instruments safely – encourage awareness of other children

• don't have children shouting or singing too loudly

• don't overdo it yourself!

Stretch and wiggle

TRACKS
1-3

Reach up high,
Reach down low,
Clap your hands with me like so.

...Stamp your feet with me like so.

...Nod your head with me like so.

...Wiggle your fingers with me like so.

...Tap your knees with me like so.

...Tickle your tummy with me like so.

What you need:
• no props are needed

How to do the activity:
• Play track 1 or sing the song to the children. Can they guess from the song what the actions are?
• Next, stand up and practise all the actions (below).
• Put the song and the actions together.

Actions:
• line 1: stand on tiptoes, stretch hands up as high as you can
• line 2: bend down, touch the floor
• line 3: do what the words say, to the beat where that is possible (verses 1, 2, 3 & 5). The percussion sounds on tracks 1 and 2 should help with keeping the beat.

FOCUS: high and low, keeping the beat, PD, CL

Stretch and wiggle: activities continued

Adapting the activity:
To make it easier: Don't worry too much about doing the actions to the beat, or, alternatively, limit the number of verses that you do, so that there are fewer words and actions to learn.
To make it more challenging: Ask the children to suggest different ways of singing the song, for example loudly/quietly, quickly/slowly or feeling lazy/excited/happy/cross.
For smaller spaces: This song also works well seated (no need to stand on tiptoe).

Other areas of learning:
Maths: Make a chart of the children's heights. Order objects according to high/higher/highest, and low/lower/lowest positions.
Understanding our world: Go outside and use chalk to draw round one another's shadows.
Expressive arts and design: Make hand or footprint pictures.
Literacy: Label body parts on a picture of a child.

Stretch and wiggle: more ideas

What you need:
- track 1
- drum, triangle, guiro, tambourine and maraca (all pictured)

How to do the activity:

Spot the instrument: Play and name all the instruments in turn. Let the children take turns to try them. Play track 1. Can the children hear and identify each instrument being played? v1: clapping, v2: drum, v3: triangle, v4: guiro, v5: tambourine, v6: maraca

Follow the instrument: Use the same instruments as above. Ask one child to play the triangle, and get everyone else to do the action from the song that goes with it (nod heads). Next, another child plays a different instrument and everyone does the correct action for that instrument. Continue the activity with the other instruments.

FOCUS: listening, timbre, PD

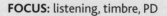

Senses song

Tune: Here we go round the mulberry bush

My senses keep me safe and sound,
I can touch and feel around,
I have a tongue to taste my food,
I have two eyes to see what's good,
I have a nose so I can smell,
I have two ears to hear as well,
My senses keep me safe and sound,
They let me know what's all around.

What you need:
• no props are needed

How to do the activity:
• Talk with the children about their five senses (touch, taste, sight, smell and hearing) and which part of the body is linked to each sense.
• There are quite a lot of words to learn in this song, so sing it nice and slowly to begin with.
• Alternatively, begin by practising the actions (below) along to track 4, and encourage the children to join in with the singing when they feel ready.
• Emphasise the beat whenever you can. For example, in line 5 tap nose to the beat.

Actions:
• line 1: thumbs up
• line 2: feel around the floor
• line 3: point to mouth
• line 4: point to eyes
• line 5: point to nose
• line 6: point to ears
• lines 7-8: thumbs up

FOCUS: keeping the beat, UW, PD

Senses song: activities continued

Adapting the activity:
To make it easier: Sing the song really slowly so the children can keep up with the words and actions, and/or cut out some of the actions.
To make it more challenging: Sing the song through very quietly, then repeat it a little louder. Keep repeating the song, getting louder each time until it is very loud (but not so loud that the children are shouting!).

Other areas of learning:
Learn about the five senses:
Understanding our world: Make feely boxes, sound bags and smelly jars. These are containers which you can't see inside, and the children have to try to identify the contents by touch, hearing or smell. Have a blindfold taste-test with fruit salad or different drinks, such as water, milk and apple juice.
PSED and physical development: Ask the children to try drawing pictures while blindfolded, then discuss the experience.

Senses song: more ideas

What you need:
- music with a strong beat

How to do the activity:
Body percussion: What sounds can the children make with their bodies? They might clap, tut, slap, rub, stamp and so on. Turn these sounds into rhythms by repeating the children's names. For example, tap the rhythm 'Amalie, Amalie, Amalie, Amalie' then repeat the rhythm, this time by tutting or stamping. You could move on to more difficult rhythms by adding surnames or taking short phrases from nursery rhymes such as 'Humpty Dumpty sat on a wall' or 'I had a little nut tree'.

Body beats: Play the music and the children make body percussion sounds to the beat.

FOCUS: rhythm, keeping the beat, PD, CL

Child-initiated learning

How to set up the activity:
Musical pictures: Lay out painting materials and paper.
• Let the children listen to music, but make sure they don't change CDs or handle electrical equipment with wet or paint-covered hands.

Look out for:
• Painting pictures of themselves or other people (using what they know in their play).
• Making pictures using hand and/or finger prints (having their own ideas).
• Responding to the music, for example by painting abstract pictures. The children might print or move paintbrushes to the beat, or they might paint fast/slowly depending on the speed of the music (choosing ways to do things and finding new ways).
• Seeking out other art materials to enhance their pictures (having their own ideas).
• Choosing specific pieces of music or even turning it off (having their own ideas).
• Use of colour and texture in their pictures (choosing ways to do things and finding new ways).

Taking it further:
• Ask the children to describe what they are doing. Do they mention body parts or senses?
• Do the children's pictures tell a story?
• Can the children print repeating patterns?
• Do their pictures have anything to do with the music they are listening to?
• Why did they choose this music to listen to, and how does it make them feel?
• What sounds can they make to go with their pictures?
• What colours have the children used? Can they tell you, and have they mixed paints to make new colours?
• If they have made hand/finger prints, what does the paint feel like on their hands? How does that change as the paint begins to dry?

Useful vocab:
• colours
• body parts
• pattern, repeat
• calm, happy, excited, sad
• wet, slimy, dry, hard

What shall we do with our friends today?

Teddy, Teddy, please say,
What shall we do with our friends today?
Teddy, Teddy, please say,
What shall we do with our friends today?
Teddy says, 'Dance!'

...Teddy says, 'Go for a walk!'

...Teddy says, 'Play a game!'

...Teddy says, 'Go to the park!'

What you need:
- a teddy
- a maraca or other instrument to shake

How to do the activity:
- Everyone sits in a circle, singing to Teddy.
- Teddy has lost his voice, so the children take turns to hold Teddy and speak for him. Teddy's words in the song lyrics are only suggestions. The children choose what Teddy says.
- Between verses, the children do Teddy's action to the sound of a maraca played by you.
- Play a definite beat for actions such as walking or dancing. For more fluid actions, make a long continuous sound with the maraca. As soon as the maraca stops, the children stop the action.
- Teddy is then passed to the next child.

FOCUS: keeping the beat, timbre, turn-taking, PD, CL

Friends: activities continued

Adapting the activity:
To make it easier: The children choose between two actions: walking (which has a definite beat) and playing a game (which doesn't have a definite beat).
To make it more challenging: Ask the children to say how to do the action. For example, they could say, 'play happily', or, 'go for a fast/slow walk'.
To make it different: Don't use Teddy. Sing to each child in turn, using their names.

Other areas of learning:
Literacy and Expressive arts and design: Make a 'year book'. All the children draw pictures of themselves and contribute positive descriptions of one another.
PSED: Discuss friendship, how we treat one another, and what makes a good friend.
Understanding the world: Find out about social etiquette and signs of friendship around the world.

Friends: more ideas

What you need:
• a teddy
• music to move to

How to do the activity:
Teddy says: One child holds Teddy and tells everyone to do an action to the music ('Teddy says dance/walk/jump/hop.'). Play the music, and the children move. Stop the music, and the children freeze. Teddy is then passed to another child and the game begins again. Try this activity with different styles of music and see how the children respond.

Silly teddy says: This game is similar to 'Teddy says', but now the children decide upon silly ways to do the actions. For example, the child holding Teddy might tell everyone to dance like a snake, walk like a giant, jump like a fairy or hop like an elephant.

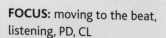

FOCUS: moving to the beat, listening, PD, CL

Family song

TRACKS 10-12

How many members in a family?
Maybe two, maybe three,
Maybe more, we shall see,
Who are the members of the family?

What you need:
• several dolls and/or cuddly toys

How to do the activity:
• For this circle song begin with one toy (the first family member) in the middle.
• Walk round in a big circle, moving feet to the beat, and sing the whole song together.
• At the end of line 4, pause to add a new family member.
• Count the family members out loud.
• Repeat the song until all the toys have been added.

FOCUS: keeping the beat, UW, PD, CL

Family song: activities continued

Adapting the activity:
To make it easier: Give the children's singing a bit of support by singing along to track 10 or 11.
To make it more challenging: Sing the song in a style that is appropriate for the family member you are adding. Let the children decide what to do. For example, if you are adding a baby brother the children might decide to sing quietly. If you are adding grandad, they might suggest singing slowly.

Other areas of learning:
PSED: In what ways are we all the same and in what ways are we different or special?
Understanding the world: Discuss the changes as we grow from babies to children to adults to elderly people.
Maths: Mark the children's birthdays on a calendar. Make a bar chart showing how many children were born in each month. Find out how old the youngest/oldest members of their families are.

Family song: more ideas

What you need:
• a tambourine (or one instrument to tap and one to shake)

How to do the activity:
The farmer's family: Play the game 'The farmer's in his den' but adapt the song to include as many different family members as you can think of. For example, the child wants a brother, the brother wants a sister, the sister wants a cousin, the cousin wants a gran, and so on.

Babies or children: The children listen for 'tapping' or 'shaking'. Tap a steady beat, and the children walk around the room. Tap slowly and the children walk slowly. Tap quickly and the children walk quickly. Shake an instrument and they move like babies, either crawling on the floor or lying on their backs kicking their feet in the air.

FOCUS: listening, timbre, keeping the beat, CL, PD

Child-initiated learning

How to set up the activity:

Musical wardrobe: Make a cardboard wardrobe or fill a cupboard or box with a varied selection of clothes.

• Try to include items of clothing that would belong to a variety of different members of the community.

• Make sure a choice of music is available to listen to.

Look out for:

• Dressing up and pretending to be different people/characters (using what they know in their play, having their own ideas).

• Role-play, including different family members (having their own ideas and using what they know in their play).

• Moving or speaking differently, depending on who they are dressed as (using what they know in their play).

• Singing or listening to music as they play (using what they know in their play).

• Making up songs as they play (having their own ideas and choosing ways to do things).

Taking it further:
- Can the children tell you who they are dressed as?
- Why have they chosen to wear these clothes?
- How do they feel dressed like this? Comfortable? Silly? Grown-up?
- Talk to the children about the music they have chosen to listen to. Perhaps they have chosen not to put music on. Ask them why.
- Give the children opportunities to add to the wardrobe and observe what they do with the new items.

ABC

Useful vocab:
- family, relative/relation
- brother, sister
- stepbrother/stepsister, half-brother/half-sister
- mother, father
- guardian, foster parents
- aunt, uncle
- cousin
- gran, grandad
- tall/taller/tallest
- short/shorter/shortest
- young/younger/youngest
- old/older/oldest

Jump out of bed

Jump out of bed, jump out of bed,
Jump out of bed in the morning,
Open your eyes and stretch up high,
And jump out of bed in the morning.

Wash your face, wash your face,
Wash your face in the morning,
Open your eyes and stretch up high,
And wash your face in the morning.

Brush your teeth, brush your teeth,
Brush your teeth in the morning,
Open your eyes and stretch up high,
And brush your teeth in the morning.

What you need:
• no props are needed

How to do the activity:
• Discuss the song words and the children's morning routines.
• Practise the actions (below). Verse 1 requires the children to jump at just the right moment, whereas the actions for verses 2 and 3 are all about keeping the beat. Try to demonstrate face washing and tooth brushing actions that have a definite feeling of the beat.
• Put the actions to the song.

Actions:
• lines 1-2:

o v1: jump forward exactly on 'jump'

o v2: circular hand movements next to cheeks

o v3: side-to-side brushing movements

• line 3: pretend to rub sleepy eyes, then stretch arms upwards

• line 4: as lines 1-2.

FOCUS: moving on cue, keeping the beat, PD, CL

Jump out of bed: activities continued

Adapting the activity:
To make it easier: Sing the song more slowly throughout, or, alternatively, stick to verse 1 only.
To make it more challenging: Tell the children that you are all very tired and sing the song very slowly. Next, tell them that you are late and must hurry, and sing the song quickly. You could also add more verses to include other things that the children do in the morning, such as 'put on your clothes' or 'eat your breakfast'.

Other areas of learning:
Literacy: Make an action-word display (jump, wash, brush and so on).
PSED: Discuss and compare the children's morning and daily routines. Learn about the importance of keeping our bodies clean, hand-washing and looking after our teeth. Make a list of everything we do to stay healthy. Go shopping for, prepare and eat some healthy food.

Jump out of bed: more ideas

What you need:
• a percussion instrument for each child
• a clock face with moveable hands
  (optional)

How to do the activity:

Alarm clocks: The children start silently. This can be tricky, so use a strategy such as laying instruments on the floor until it is time to play. On your cue, the children play their instruments suddenly and very loudly – the alarm. The cue could simply be, 'Ready, steady, WAKE UP!' and the 'alarm' goes off. Alternatively, you could move the hands of a large clock, and when they reach, say, 8 o'clock the children play.

Sleepy music: Firstly you pretend to be asleep and the children play their instruments gently. This is the 'sleepy music'. Then you pretend to wake up and the children play much louder. This is 'wide-awake music'.

FOCUS: following a cue, loud and quiet, PD, M

Tick-tock

TRACKS
16-18

Tick-tock, tick-tock
Goes the grandfather clock,
Time for breakfast,
It's 8 o'clock.

...Time for lunch,
It's 12 o'clock.

...Time for dinner,
It's 5 o'clock.

...Time for bed,
It's 7 o'clock.

What you need:
• a clock face with moveable hands
• a percussion instrument for each child (optional)

How to do the activity:
• Make sure that the children know what a grandfather clock is.
• Practise the actions (below). Encourage the children to try and keep in time with you.
• Practise the chime actions with a clock. Turn the hands to 8 o'clock and the children clap eight times. Repeat with different times.
• Now sing the song. Turn the clock to the correct time before you start each verse.

Actions:
• lines 1-2: point index fingers upwards and make side-to-side tick-tock movements with forearms

• lines 3-4: tap wrist (watch)

• between verses: clap the correct number of chimes

FOCUS: keeping the beat, CL, M

Tick-tock: activities continued

Adapting the activity:
To make it easier: Leave out the clock chimes between the verses. Everyone simply sings the song.
To make it more challenging: Ask the children to suggest other times of the day to sing about, for example snack time or home time.
To make it different: Instead of hand actions, use percussion instruments to make a steady tick-tock sound throughout the song, and to play the chimes between verses.

Other areas of learning:
Understanding the world: What else happens at different times of the day? For example, when does the post arrive, or a parent get home from work? What time does it get light/dark?
Maths: Use a stopwatch to time the children doing different tasks. For example, how long does it take to tidy up or put on our coats or listen to a story?
PSED: What is the children's favourite time of day and why?

Tick-tock: more ideas

What you need:
- a percussion instrument to tap, such as a tone block

- a triangle

How to do the activity:

Follow the clock: Tap a steady beat on your percussion instrument and the children do the tick-tock hand action from the song, keeping exactly to your beat. Make your clock go a bit faster and the children must keep up. Make your clock go slowly and the children slow down too. Pause, and the children pause their actions. How carefully are the children watching and listening? Can you catch them out?

What's the time?: The children take turns to play clock chimes on the triangle (any number from 1 to 12). After each child has played, the others (who have been silently counting the chimes) say what time it is.

FOCUS: keeping the beat, fast and slow, playing a solo, PD, M

Child-initiated learning

How to set up the activity:
Bedtime: Set up an area of the room where the children can put dolls and cuddly toys to bed.
• Let the children listen to music as they play, and set out some books and percussion instruments nearby.
• If you include a bath and towels, make sure the children don't change CDs or handle electrical equipment with wet hands.

Look out for:
• Role-play, taking the role of mum or dad at bath and bedtime: bathing and drying dolls, changing nappies, dressing the dolls in pyjamas (using what they know in their play).
• Deciding how to build beds for the toys and collecting the materials they need (choosing ways to do things).
• Debating what constitutes a 'correct' bedtime routine and learning that things differ from household to household (using what they know in their play and choosing ways to do things).
• Finding different ways to make baby comfortable in bed, reading to baby and singing lullabies to send baby to sleep (using what they know in their play and choosing ways to do things).
• Choosing appropriate music for baby to listen to as they go to sleep (having their own ideas).
• Waking baby up with a percussion alarm clock (using what they know in their play and choosing ways to do things).

Taking it further:
• Ask the children about the music they are listening to. Why have they chosen it?
• Can the children use the percussion instruments to make sleepy music and wide-awake music?
• Talk to the children about the books they have read to baby.
• Tell the children that baby is crying and observe what they do.
• Invite a parent to bring their baby in to meet the children, to talk about feeding, bathtime and bedtime routines. Afterwards, observe if there is more interest in the 'bedtime' area, and/or a change in the way the children play there.

Useful vocab:
• bathtime, bedtime
• lullaby
• soothe
• sleeping/awake
• settled/unsettled

Musical mirrors

TRACK 19

Tune: March from The Nutcracker by Pyotr Ilyich Tchaikovsky

The Nutcracker ballet was written in 1892 by the Russian composer Tchaikovsky who is famous for orchestral music, including his other ballets, *Swan Lake* and *Sleeping Beauty*.

When you listen to the music you will hear some musical themes (or tunes) recurring at different points. This is the structure of the music, and the actions on p39 help to point this out to the children.

Because it was written as dance music, the March really lends itself to movement, so another way to enjoy the music would be to simply ask the children to move to it. They could march, jump, dance, wiggle, or choose their own movements and respond freely to the music.

What you need:
• March from *The Nutcracker* music
• a mirror (full-length if possible)

How to do the activity:
• Let the children take turns to look in the mirror and observe what happens to their reflection when they move.
• Put the mirror away and ask the children to copy (mirror) your actions, for example, raising and lowering your arms.
• Next, introduce the music and actions (below), moving in time to the music with the children mirroring you as closely as they can.

Actions:
• These actions highlight the structure of the music: **0:00** tap head then shoulders (x4); **0:07** wave hands from side to side; **0:13** tap head then shoulders (x4); **0:19** wave hands from side to side; **0:25** wave hands all the way down to touch toes and back up again; **0:31** repeat toe-touching action; **0:38** tap head then shoulders (x4); **0:44** wave hands from side to side; **0:50** tap head then shoulders (x4); **0:56** wave hands from side to side.

FOCUS: keeping the beat, structure, PD, UW

Musical mirrors: activities continued

Adapting the activity:
To make it easier: Say what you are doing out loud: 'Tap, tap, tap, tap...', 'Wave, wave, wave, wave...' and so on. Watch the children carefully, and continue with each action until all the children have managed to join in.
To make it different and/or more difficult: Interpret the music in your own way with different actions, still moving to the beat. Try changing the mood of your actions to happy (e.g. skipping), sad (e.g. shaking head), grumpy (e.g. stamping foot) or excited (e.g. jumping). Choose a child to be the leader and let everyone else mirror them.

Other areas of learning:
Literacy: Make a 'funny faces' display. Draw faces with different expressions and label them with words that describe how we feel: happy, sad, grumpy, excited and so on.
Maths: Introduce symmetry using pictures, shapes, paper-folding and mirrors.
Understanding the world: This music is from a ballet. Find out about different forms of dance from around the world and listen to the music that goes with them.

Musical mirrors: more ideas

What you need:
- scarves, ribbons or strips of crêpe paper
- March from *The Nutcracker* music

How to do the activity:

Musical scarves: Wave scarves to the music. Can the children wave them to the beat? Introduce different moods: wave the scarves calmly/cheerfully/gloomily/lazily/furiously/peacefully and so on. Encourage the children to continue listening and responding to the music as they do this.

Happy singers: Sing a really familiar song in different moods or styles. For example, try singing 'Twinkle, twinkle' really grumpily (this can be very funny if you exaggerate it) and then sing it very sadly, then excitedly, and finish with a happy version.

FOCUS: keeping the beat, PD, PSED

Can you play?

TRACKS 20-25

Tune: Twinkle, twinkle little star (adapted)

Solo version: Can you play just like me?
                 Listen, listen carefully.

Group version: We will play just like you,
                 Show us, show us what to do.

What you need:
• a percussion instrument for everyone

How to do the activity:
• This song encourages the children to play instruments in different ways: loud, slow, happy, lazy, excited etc.
• There are two versions of the song: one for a solo singer, and another for everyone to sing. Both versions are followed by the same percussion game.
• **Solo version (tracks 20-22):** Sing the song to the children, then play your instrument loudly while the children listen (and keep their own instruments as quiet as they can!). The children then copy what you did.
• Repeat the whole activity, including the song, several times, playing differently (fast, calmly etc.) each time.
• **Group version (tracks 23-25):** Let a child lead the percussion playing. Everyone sings the group version of the song, then the leader plays his/her instrument and everyone copies.
• Repeat until all the children have had a turn to be the leader.

FOCUS: loud and quiet, fast and slow, PSED, PD

Can you play? activities continued

Adapting the activity:
To make it easier: Stick to the solo version, so the children only have to copy you.
To make it more difficult: Give individual children the opportunity to sing the solo version.
For larger spaces: Turn this into a movement activity, without the instruments. Sing, 'Can you move just like me? Watch and listen carefully.' and tiptoe, march, skip, crawl, jump on the spot, hop or even stay very still. Sing the group version of the song, and let the children take turns at being the leader: 'We will move just like you...'.

Other areas of learning:
PSED: What makes the children feel happy/sad/grumpy/excited, and how can we affect other people's moods?
Understanding our world: Play a listening game. Make recordings of everyday sounds, such as a clock, a running tap and footsteps. Can the children identify them?

Can you play? more ideas

What you need:
- March from *The Nutcracker* music
- a percussion instrument for each child

How to do the activity:
Play along: Play the instruments along to the music. Can the children play to the beat? Stop the music, swap instruments and begin again.

Peek-a-boo: Hide your face, then peek-a-boo with a happy expression. This is the children's cue to play their instruments happily. Peek-a-boo again, this time with a sad expression, and the children play sad sounds. While you are hiding the children must keep their instruments silent. Surprise the children with lots of different expressions/moods. The children could also take turns at doing the peek-a-boos with a partner.

FOCUS: keeping the beat, timbre, playing on cue, CL, UW

Child-initiated learning

How to set up the activity:
Music corner: Designate a special place to store all of the instruments and props that you use for the activities in this book.
• Make sure the children know where the music corner is, and that they can have access to the equipment whenever they want to use it in their play.

Look out for:
• Recreating the activities from this book (using what they know in their play).
• Playing on their own, in pairs or in groups (being willing to have a go).
• Organising themselves and one another (having their own ideas).
• Adapting songs, games and rhymes that they know (using what they already know and finding new ways).
• Inventing new songs, games and rhymes (having their own ideas).
• Playing the percussion instruments in different styles or moods (choosing ways to do things and finding new ways).
• Choosing music to listen and/or move to (choosing ways to do things).

Taking it further:
• Can the children adapt their activities by imagining a particular audience or occasion? For example, can they sing quietly because Gran is sleeping, or play faster because your train is leaving soon?
• Discuss the songs and activities with the children. Which do they like best and why? Are some easy or difficult? Do they enjoy them more as a large group or on their own?
• Talk to the children about the music they are listening to. Why have they chosen it and how does it make them feel?
• Ask the children to choose music for a particular person or reason. For example, what would they choose to dance to at a party, or to cheer up a grumpy brother, or soothe an angry sister?

ABC

Useful vocab:
• loud/quiet
• fast/slow
• calm, cheerful, gloomy, lazy, furious, peaceful
• names of percussion instruments
• shake, tap, scrape

Useful resources

Music:

Here are some ideas for instrumental music that suggests different moods or feelings:

Classical music:
- *Lullaby* by Johannes Brahms
- In the Hall of the Mountain King from *Peer Gynt Suite No. 1* by Edvard Grieg
- Morning from *Peer Gynt Suite No. 1* by Edvard Grieg

Film soundtracks:
- *Finding Nemo* (main title) (Thomas Newman)
- *The Incredibles* (Michael Giacchino)
- *Monsters Inc.* (Randy Newman)

Websites:

www.acblack.com

www.musicalsteps.co.uk

www.oxfam.org.uk (Click on 'teachers' then on 'Early Years' for resources and activities about friendship and children around the world.)

Non-fiction books:

Your Body (Brenda Stones, Kingfisher Readers)

The 5 Senses (Nuria Roca and Rosa Maria Curto, Barron's Educational Series)

A life like mine (UNICEF) How Children Live Around the World (Children just like me) (DK ELT/schools)

Little topic book of ourselves (Liz Powlay, Featherstone Education)

Fiction books:

The good mood hunt (Hiawyn Oram, OUP)

Badger's bad mood (Hiawyn Oram, Picture Lions)

Peepo (Janet & Allan Ahlberg, Puffin)

The Nutcracker (Emma Helbrough, Usborne Picture Books)